Edward J. Hawkins

My New Easter Friends

ISBN:

978-621-434-130-6 (paperback)
978-621-434-131-3 (hardback)
978-621-434-132-0 (ebook)

Published by:

OMNIBOOK CO.

99 Wall Street, Suite 118

New York, NY 10005

USA

+1-866-216-9965

www.omnibookcompany.com

For e-book purchase: Kindle on Amazon, Barnes and Noble

Book purchase: Amazon.com, Barnes & Noble,
and www.omnibookcompany.com

Omnibook titles may be purchased in bulk for educational, business, fund-raising, or sales promotional use. For more information please e-mail info@omnibookcompany.com

Visit the author's website at www.StoriesOfEd.com

"Hello, my name is **Turtle**. What is your name?"

"My name is **Bunny**, but my friends call me Hopper," said **Bunny**.

"And my friends call me SP." said **Turtle**.

"What does that stand for? Inquired **Bunny**.

"Slow Poke" responded **Turtle**.

"So little **Bunny**, where are you going?" said **Turtle**.

"I am hopping over to see my friends for Easter."

"That is great, may I tag along and we can talk."

"Oh, I suppose, but you might slow me down."

Turtle thought about it and reflected for a moment, "I will hurry as fast as I can, as I have four legs," he told **Bunny**.

1

2

"I want to see my friends and bring them something." said **Bunny**, "So I brought along this basket to fill with things along the way and it is rather big for me to carry." continuing his thought process **Bunny** continued, "Perhaps you could hold it on your back for me?"

Turtle again thought about the question, "Well as long as it is not too heavy for me, I will do it for you my new friend."

The two of them continued their walk along the path on a beautiful day. Then **Turtle** believed he saw something brightly colored ahead. "I think I see an Easter egg under that bush over there, about two o'clock."

4

Bunny took the basket off Turtle's back and said, "wait here," and hopped over to the bright blue egg. "This is nice," said Bunny "my friends will like a bright blue egg on Easter." Bunny hopped back to Turtle and put the bright blue egg into the basket and loaded it back onto Turtles back.

That was a nice find, Bunny thought and told his new friend as the two continued down the road to Bunny's destination, with Turtle doing most of the talking. Soon, Turtle spotted some more colored eggs and told Bunny.

5

6

"Wow, how sweet is that?" exclaimed **Bunny**. **Bunny** once again lifted the basket onto the ground and hopped over to where the eggs sat and this time there were two eggs--one green and one purple. Then **Bunny** spotted three more eggs not far from the green and purple eggs. So, then he returned the green and purple eggs to the basket and then hopped over to the other three eggs he had spotted and these eggs had designs all over them.

Bunny picked up two, hopped back over to the basket, and carefully placed them into the basket before going back for the third egg. Wow, thought **Bunny** now how many eggs do I have? Well, I have the blue one that **Turtle** first saw, and the green and purple eggs that **Turtle** later saw and that makes three eggs.

In addition, I have the three designed eggs that I found for a total of six eggs in my basket. **Bunny** told **Turtle** of the six eggs in the basket and what do you think **Turtle** said? "of course," he said, I know, I know, they are on my back and they are starting to get heavy." "So, how much further to go?" asked **Turtle**.

12

"Not much further, in fact there is the house now," stated **Bunny** to **Turtle**. I will introduce you to my friends when we get there. With the weight of the basket on **Turtle**, it was after all, a little slower than **Bunny** would have liked, but soon they were at the door of **Bunny's** friends. **Bunny** knocked and the door opened up and **Bunny** was greeted with a friendly "Well, hello Hopper, how have you been?" "Great," Said **Bunny**, "now let me introduce you to my new friend **Turtle**.

"This is **Turtle**, and he has helped me with this basket for your family."

"Well, thank you very much Hopper and **Turtle**, said **Bunny's** friend." Then **Bunny** turned to **Turtle** and introduced them to his friends "**Turtle**, these are my friends Zack and Sarah and their new baby Ben."

They all had a wonderful Easter brunch and **Turtle** and **Bunny** went back home and continued to be good friends for many years.

CPSIA information can be obtained
at www.ICGtesting.com
Printed in the USA
BVHW021020010321
601383BV00013B/112